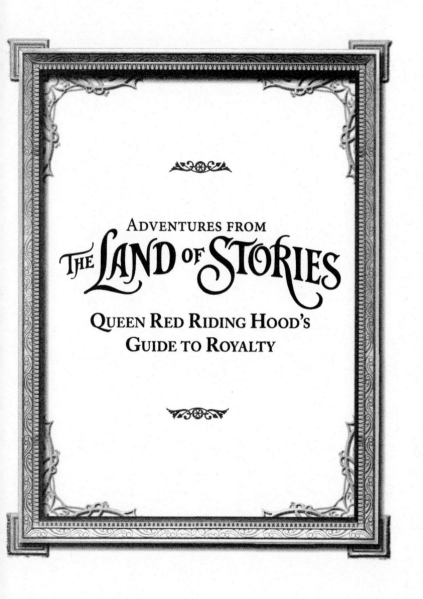

Adventures from The Land of Stories

Queen Red Riding Hood's Guide to Royalty

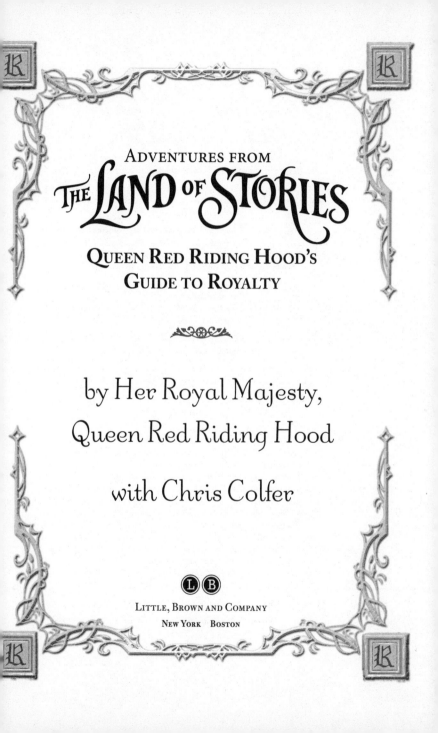

ADVENTURES FROM
The LAND of STORIES

QUEEN RED RIDING HOOD'S GUIDE TO ROYALTY

by Her Royal Majesty,
Queen Red Riding Hood

with Chris Colfer

L **B**

LITTLE, BROWN AND COMPANY
NEW YORK   BOSTON

Little, Brown and Company
Hachette Book Group
1290 Avenue of the Americas, New York, NY 10104
Visit us at lb-kids.com

Originally published in *Adventures from the Land of Stories* in November 2015
First stand-alone edition: July 2017

Little, Brown and Company is a division of Hachette Book Group, Inc. The Little, Brown name and logo are trademarks of Hachette Book Group, Inc.

The publisher is not responsible for websites (or their content) that are not owned by the publisher.

Library of Congress Cataloging-in-Publication Data
Names: Colfer, Chris, 1990– author.
Title: The Land of Stories : Queen Red Riding Hood's guide to royalty /
by Her Royal Majesty Queen Red Riding Hood ; with Chris Colfer.
Other titles: Queen Red Riding Hood's guide to royalty
Description: First stand-alone edition. | New York ; Boston : Little, Brown and Company,
[2016] | "First published in Adventures from the Land of Stories in November 2015." |
Summary: "Queen Red Riding Hood from the Land of Stories gives advice and makes
observations on how to rule." —Provided by publisher.
Identifiers: LCCN 2015047350 | ISBN 9780316383363 (paper over board)
Subjects: | CYAC: Fairy tales—Fiction. | Characters in literature—Fiction. | Kings,
queens, rulers, etc.—Fiction. | Humorous stories.
Classification: LCC PZ7.C677474 Laj 2016 | DDC [Fic]—dc23
LC record available at https://lccn.loc.gov/2015047350

ISBNs: 978-0-316-38336-3 (hardcover), 978-0-316-38338-7 (ebook)

Printed in the United States of America

LSC-C

10 9 8 7 6 5 4 3 2 1

To my beloved Charlie:

Little girls are told if they kiss a frog, they may get a prince.

I kissed a prince and wound up with a frog.

Then again, I've never been good with instructions.

But I wouldn't have it any other way.

I love you.

Introduction

The Prince and Me

Fellow Hoodians, admirers, royal subjects, and royal rejects. Thank you for choosing my first book, *Queen Red Riding Hood's Guide to Royalty*, as your reading selection. I can't imagine the anticipation, enthusiasm, and admiration coursing through your feeble bodies as you hold your very own copy. Before you excite yourself to the point of needing medical attention, I must thank you for the hours and/or days I assume you waited in line to purchase it.

And to ease those uncontrollable thoughts of unconditional gratitude, just know the pleasure is all mine!

I'm certain your simple minds are all wondering the same thing. "Why would our astonishing queen go out of her way to write a book?" I thought the same thing when I first sat down to write it. The truth is, wherever I go, there are always crowds of devoted followers asking me the same questions: "Your Majesty, how do you do it? How do you manage to govern a prosperous kingdom, endure countless adventures, and maintain such beauty and poise so effortlessly?" Since I do not have the time (or the patience) to respond to each individual, I decided to compile my numerous secrets into this book to answer all your pressing questions at once. You're welcome.

The idea first came to me one evening while I was lounging in my newly refurnished library. I had just finished a charming and silly little play called *Hamhead* by William Shakyfruit—excuse me, *Hamlet* by *William Shakespeare*. I was looking for another humorous read from the Otherworld when I came upon a delightful book called *The Prince* by Nicole Macarena—or was it Niccolò Machiavelli? Well, whatever her name was, I thought it was a splendid story! In summary, *The Prince* was a guide to *monarchy*! Isn't that marvelous? It gave helpful hints on managing a government, making the proper alliances, and keeping respectable appearances. The best part of reading the book was realizing *I've been doing everything correctly since my coronation!* Although I doubt that surprises you.

However helpful Ms. Machiavelli's words were, I couldn't help feeling her book was a little outdated. It may have had its purpose at one point in time, but it isn't relevant to politics today—just like ruffled bloomers (more on that in my next book, *Queen Red Riding Hood's Guide to Style*).

Since I am the beacon of ideal leadership, I felt it was my duty to give the seminal classic a makeover! Who else could possibly be qualified for the job? For the next several minutes, or however long it takes to write a book, I will combine the concepts of *The Prince* with the constant requests of my people and create my own guide for future royals to follow and future royalists to treasure. Again, you're welcome.

History will see this guide as one of the greatest literary achievements of our time, because as queen, I have control over what history remembers. So, curl up with your copy in a cozy corner of your own library. Give your servants a list of meaningless tasks so that you aren't bothered. If you have children, tell your nannies to keep them at a ballroom's-length distance. Give your House of Parliament, Congress, or Progress the day off. Relax and enjoy this historical triumph!

Chapter 1

Beneath the Hood

I believe that, before taking advice from someone, it's important to know exactly whom you're taking the advice from. So before we dive into matters of economy, politics, image, charity, and all the other nonsense a king or queen deals with, it's important that I introduce you to the real me.

Naturally, this may confuse your delicate heads. After all, my profile is engraved on every coin, statues of me stand on every street corner, and I'm certain my portraits decorate your modest homes. You couldn't be unfamiliar with me if you tried! However, the familiarity I speak of has nothing to do with my exquisite appearance: I'm talking about the woman *beneath the hood*.

For the first time in my reign, I'm going to give you, my people, a glimpse into my personal life, my mind, my heart, and my impeccable soul. My past may be one of the greatest stories ever told, but rarely do I speak about it myself—unless you work at the castle; then you may hear me reminiscing two or three times a day.

There is more to my story than you realize, and once I share it with you, I believe you'll admire me even more than you do now. Yes, it's possible.

This will be hard to believe, but I was once as you are now. Just like Cinderella, I was an exceptional young girl cursed by *humble beginnings*. I was born to two simple farmers in the Northern Kingdom, long before the C.R.A.W.L. Revolution separated us from the north (more on that in a moment—please stay focused!). My parents mistreated me horribly, which is why I've chosen to distance myself from them today.

It saddens me to tell you that my childhood was filled with misery. Every morning I was forced out of bed before noon and ordered to do horrific tasks like *chores* and *schoolwork*. I was assaulted by *rules* and *standards*. I was restricted with *curfews* and *bedtimes*. Every day, my mother and father would say horrible things to me, like "you can't have that" and "no."

Despite my declarations that I deserved much better treatment, my parents ignored me, and the nightmare continued. As an only child, I had to endure it all alone. My parents must have known deep down I was extraordinary, because whenever I asked if I was going to have any brothers or sisters, they'd reply, "You're enough."

Unlike Cinderella, I did not let my unfortunate origins affect my sanity—*you'll never see me talking to mice!* Despite the mistreatment I received from my parents, I never stopped believing I was meant for bigger things (and I'm not talking about that summer when I gained weight and needed new clothes).

My weekend visits to my granny's house were my only sanctuary from my terrible home life. Granny never treated me like a servant or a prisoner but saw me as the exceptional human being I am. She treated me to candies, toys, and naps. She offered me the compassion and respect my early years were missing, always saying encouraging things like "have another cookie" and "yes." I honestly don't know how I would have survived without her.

Granny made my first hooded coat. She chose a fabric the exact color of my name and christened me *Little Red Riding Hood*. I think the coat helped her remember who I was when I showed up at her house. Poor Granny has never had the best memory.

In a serendipitous twist of fate, the people of my future kingdom were also suffering. The villages and farms of the Northern Kingdom were constantly under attack by wolves, with no salvation in sight.

Queen Snow White's stepmother was on the throne at the time. She was so busy with her magic mirrors and attempted murder, she ignored her people's requests for protection—hence the name she is now remembered by: the Evil Queen.

When the Little Boy Who Cried Wolf was murdered, it was the last straw. The villagers and farmers banded together and started the C.R.A.W.L. (Citizens' Riots Against Wolf Liberty) Revolution with their sights set on establishing their own kingdom away from the Evil Queen's jurisdiction.

My granny was very active in the revolution and caught a nasty cold during one of the demonstrations—a hunger strike, if I recall. We knew she needed to get her strength up, so my mother packed a basket of goods and sent me to deliver it to Granny's house on the other side of the woods.

I would like to take a moment to reiterate this: *My mother sent her only daughter into the woods alone in the midst of wolf attacks and a revolution!* See what I mean? Terrible parenting! It was during this journey to Granny's house when I infamously encountered the Big Bad Wolf himself, and the rest of my extraordinary story took place.

While we're on the subject, I have something to get off my chest. Over the years, I have been criticized for telling the Big Bad Wolf that I was headed to my granny's house, followed by directions of how to get there. However, this should not be a testament to *my* judgment, but once again to *bad parenting*. My mother and father never sat me down and said, "Red, if you meet a wolf in the woods, don't give him your itinerary." If they actually cared about my well-being, they would have properly warned me.

And another thing! As I said earlier, my granny was involved in several revolutionary protests in those days—she was always dressing up in weird outfits! So when I walked into her bedroom and saw the Big Bad Wolf lying in her bed, I had no reason to believe it wasn't her! Any logical girl would have thought the same thing.

Phew! I'll sleep much better knowing I've put that in writing. I assume you know what happened next, but I'll tell you anyway.

The Big Bad Wolf gobbled me up in one bite and I met up with Granny in his stomach. We spent two days inside the wolf's belly, but it really wasn't as unpleasant as one would imagine. Once we got used to the smell, it was rather warm and comfortable. Luckily, Granny had managed to grab a deck of cards as the wolf swallowed her, so we improved our gambling skills as we awaited rescue.

Eventually, my parents grew concerned and asked a hunter to help them look for me. The hunter found the wolf at Granny's house in the exact spot he had eaten me. Apparently Granny and I were too much for him to digest and he was experiencing a miserable food coma. The hunter killed the wolf with one slice of his axe, and Granny and I fell out of him like candy out of a piñata.

By the time we were saved, the C.R.A.W.L. Revolution was over. The villagers and farmers had successfully separated from the Northern Kingdom. All they needed now was a name for the kingdom . . . *and someone to lead them!*

Word quickly spread through our unsupervised and unnamed kingdom about Granny's and my brave encounter with the Big Bad Wolf (probably because I told everyone who would listen). We were called before the C.R.A.W.L. Committee—which consisted of a farmer, a shepherdess, three village elders, and a chicken (I'm still not sure how the chicken was appointed). They were mesmerized by our story and felt we embodied the kingdom's struggles, so they asked Granny to be queen.

"Who? Me?" Granny said. "I'm not sure I'm up for all that pomp and circumstance. I don't have the hips for it."

"Then what about Billy Bopkins?" the farmer asked the committee. "He's got great leadership qualities and he's more respected than anyone else in my village."

"Billy Bopkins is a goat," the shepherdess said.

"Since when do we discriminate?" the farmer said.

"Perhaps someone *young*?" Granny suggested. "Forming a kingdom is going to take a lot of energy."

It was one of those moments that exist only in legends, fables, and Shakyfruit plays. The committee all turned and looked at me in unison, as if their eyes were drawn to me by a higher power. And by the way, it wasn't because I was jumping up and down, waving my arms above my head, and shouting, *"Pick me! Pick me! Pick me!"* That is a vicious rumor I would like to put to rest.

I knew I had to act fast before the committee put the kingdom's fate in the wrong hooves. I stepped forward, placed one hand over my heart and raised the other into the air, and recited my sacred oath as queen.

"I, fabulous Little Red Riding Hood, solemnly swear to govern this kingdom, to serve its people, and to guide it to prosperity, so help me God."

The committee stared at me with very blank expressions. I may not have been their first choice, but all of them were in awe of my natural instinct to take initiative. Clearly I was born to rule.

"All in favor of Queen Red Riding Hood, say aye," the shepherdess said.

The committee members looked at one another and shrugged. They couldn't name another candidate, because I was undoubtedly the best option.

"Aye!" the committee said in unison.

From that moment forward, Little Red Riding Hood ceased to exist. I became *Her Royal Majesty, Queen Red Riding Hood!* The world has been a better place ever since.

"What were you planning to name the kingdom?" Granny asked the committee.

"Well, it's in between all the other kingdoms, so why not call it the In-Between Kingdom?" the farmer asked.

"Absolutely not!" the shepherdess argued. "It should be called the C.R.A.W.L. Kingdom."

The rest of the committee liked this idea, except the chicken. I wasn't thrilled with the idea, either, so I politely cleared my throat before any eggs were laid in objection.

"Since I'm queen, shouldn't it be my decision?" I asked. "Hold on—*I'm the queen!* I don't need to ask your permission. I'll name the kingdom myself!"

Naming the kingdom was the hardest decision I've ever had to make as queen. I wanted our home to have the most magnificent name in the world. I wanted it to be something the people could be proud of and inspired by, something that could make all the other kingdoms envious.

"I've got it," I said. "We'll name it the *Red Riding Hood Kingdom!*"

The committee scrunched their brows, opened their mouths, and stared at me with large eyes. Obviously they were so impressed it rendered them speechless! Even my harshest critics couldn't deny the *Red Riding Hood Kingdom* had a nice ring to it. (The kingdom has since been renamed a few times, but we won't get into that.)

My first hours as queen were highly efficient. First, I assembled a group of royal subjects to assist me during my reign—the third Little Pig, BaaBaa Blacksheep, Miss Muffet, Jack Horner, the Three Blind Mice, the Little Old Woman from the Shoe Inn, and Granny, of course! Second, I demanded a wall be built around our kingdom so my people would never have to live in fear of wolves again (that one was Granny's idea).

Unfortunately, no proper venues had been built to host the coronation yet—so it took place in an old barn. Instead of jewelry and robes, I was crowned with a bucket and a dog's blanket. Instead of adoring citizens shouting "long live the queen," my crowning was followed by approving *baa*s, *neigh*s, and *moo*s of the sheep, horses, and cows living in the barn. A lesser monarch would have let the experience belittle them, but it only influenced my third and most important act as queen: *building the home and the wardrobe I deserved!*

The best builders and designers were brought in from all over the kingdom and created my glorious castle and fantastic clothes. I finally lived and looked like a queen should. Peasants traveled from miles around just to get a glimpse of their beautiful ruler and pay their respects, not to mention shower me with compliments!

At last, I was leading the life I was destined for! Unfortunately, not *everyone* was as enthusiastic.

"They elected you *what*?" Father asked when I broke the news.

"Dad, I just told you I'm the queen now!" I said. "And from now on you must address me as *Your Royal Majesty, Queen Red Riding Hood* when you're in my presence."

"I don't understand," Mother said. (Then again, she never did.)

"Mom, I'm wearing twenty pounds of jewelry and arrived in a golden carriage. What part of *queen* don't you understand?"

"Are you still going to live with us?" Father asked.

"Of course not," I said. "They've built me a castle in the center of town."

"So are we coming to live with you?" Mother asked.

"Why? So you can continue your exploitation?" I said. "Absolutely not. As queen, I can't waste an ounce of my strength battling your mind games."

"Mind games?" Father said. "Red, we love you, but you're too young to be a *queen*."

It was the single most hurtful thing anyone has ever said to me in my entire life. There I was, standing before them as their chosen sovereign, gracing their presence as a courtesy, and they only considered me a *child*. My disdain was evident by the scowl and stomps that followed.

"All right, Red. You're *the queen*," Mother said with air quotations I didn't appreciate. "But when you're done, dinner is at seven o'clock."

I headed out of the house but paused in the doorway. I looked back at my parents, hoping to see a sign of remorse or hear an apology for all the heartache they had caused me over the years. No such indication came.

"You shall never clip my wings again," I said. "I'll send one of my handmaidens to collect my things— that's right, I have *handmaidens*."

I never saw my parents again—well, besides the third Sunday of every month when they come to the castle for an awkward dinner with Granny, but that's practically *never* in royal standards. I've lived peacefully in my castle, free from their damaging clutches, ever since. (Except for those brief times I wasn't queen and lived elsewhere, but we won't get into that, either.)

There you have it—my complete story from my own lips. Your queen has lived a difficult and challenging life, but she's only become stronger, wiser, and prettier because of it. Now that you've heard my inspiring story of survival, you should have no reservation about following my advice in the rest of this guide.

My God, I've been at this for hours! Don't expect the following chapters to be as long as this. I still have a kingdom to look after, you know. Now, if you'll excuse me, I'm going to treat myself to a nice hot bubble bath.

Reminiscing is exhausting, especially when you've lived a life as significant as mine. It's just like Shakyfruit once wrote: "Uneasy is the head that wears a hood."

The Royal
A P P

Appearance

Performance

and Perception

Chapter 2

Image Is Everything

Without question, the most important and sacred thing to a ruler is his or her *image*! Any monarch who says "the well-being of their people and kingdom is what matters most to me" is only saying that to gain approval and avoid a revolution. Trust me—*I've been there!*

Don't be fooled by the poor saps who claim "what's inside your heart is what truly matters"—that is an absolute lie! The *outside* definitely outweighs the *inside* when you sit on a throne. You must be taken seriously if you want to survive as a monarch, and that starts with your appearance. No one is going to respect or admire a pudgy slob. You must look and act the part if you expect to get anywhere . . . or simply stay exactly where you are.

To your people, you represent God, because she chose you to lead them. (One might argue that a farmer, a shepherdess, three old folks, and a chicken chose me; to that, I say, "God works in mysterious ways!") Therefore, you must represent God by being nothing less than perfection in the public eye. In a way, you must be God-like yourself.

I believe anyone can achieve this immortal facade with three easy steps I've created. I call them *the Royal APP: appearance, performance, and perception.*

Appearance

Sometimes a king or queen is the only glimpse of a kingdom the outside world is privy to. Consequently, the condition of your government, economy, and citizens will be assessed on your looks alone. In other words, your book will be judged by its cover, *so make it pretty!*

Let's have a moment of honesty. I'm the queen of a farming country; if I accurately represented my kingdom, I would be walking around in a bonnet with rural animals running in circles around my feet. *Not going to happen!* Luckily, as queen it's my duty to bring class and respectability to my kingdom's image. I can't let the world think we're a bunch of staff-carrying pig breeders—even if we are. That's why I've chosen to shape my appearance after my kingdom's *potential*, not its truth. And I strongly recommend you do the same.

I believe the Red Riding Hood Kingdom will live up to its name and become a beautiful, wealthy, and cosmopolitan nation. So *that's* how I dress, and it's benefited us greatly. My sense of style is why our kingdom has such good relations with the neighboring countries. Everyone who sees me imagines the kingdom is as strong, rich, and sophisticated as I am. (And the fact that we grow over two-thirds of the world's food doesn't hurt, either.)

The better I look to the world, the better my kingdom looks to the world, and the better my kingdom looks to the world, the better I look to my own people. It's a wonderful and enjoyable cycle that furthers my superiority.

So, as anyone can see, my need for nice things is entirely selfless. The gowns, the jewelry, the castles, the parties, and everything about my lavish lifestyle are for the prosperity of my people. I endure it all for *them*.

Performance

Every ruler must learn to act sooner than later. As difficult as it may be, you must never seem tired, angry, hungry, envious, or anything but perfectly comfortable.

Any trace of humanity will be seen as weakness, and visible weaknesses can be dangerous to a ruler.

Never say "I have to use the little girls room" or "I need a nap" or "I'm going to start throwing the babies I get asked to kiss if I don't get out of here!" All statements can be replaced with the simple phrase "Now I must be alone to think about matters of the kingdom." Or, if you're really desperate, like when a villager won't stop talking, you can interrupt them with "Pardon me, I forgot about a very important matter I need to address this moment." No one can ever fault you for saying this, and it's a guaranteed way to get some much-needed alone time.

Of course, we both know the truth of our humanity. There are some days we can't help looking like the humans we are. Even God's chosen ones become ill, fatigued, or puffy from time to time. Thankfully, I have a solution for these times of need: *jewelry!*

Save your finest and shiniest jewels for the times you aren't feeling your best. When people are blinded by your diamond necklace, they'll never see the circles under your eyes. No one can say you look any less like a million gold coins if you're wearing something literally worth a million gold coins.

Perception

This is the most important part of the Royal APP. If you play your cards right, a solid *perception* will make your *appearance* and *performance* much easier to manage.

One out of ten citizens may have the privilege of seeing me in the flesh during their lifetime. So how do you make your presence known throughout your kingdom when physical encounters are rare? The answer is simple and rulers have been doing it since the beginning of time: *tributes!*

There's a reason monarchs display so many portraits and statues of themselves throughout their kingdom. *Narcissism*, obviously—but if they're smart, they'll use their narcissism *strategically*. The trick is getting people to know "you" without ever meeting *you*. I use the adorable quotations because the "you" that you want known may not be who you actually are. I'll explain....

A respectable and admirable public opinion is achieved by a light dose of brainwashing. Harsh, but true—just like overhead lighting. But don't worry, the peasants are so wrapped up in their peasantry they have no clue it's even happening. Getting them to understand the concept of *washing* has been a challenge alone; I doubt their tender minds could recognize the subliminal messages strategically staged around the kingdom to subconsciously alter their judgment. I don't even understand what I just wrote.

It's not a secret that most kings and queens force artists to alter their appearance in artwork. You should see what real monarchs look like in comparison to their portraits. *Woof!* If the art was truthful, once the artist finished their noses there would be no paint left!

But besides improving their attractiveness, most leaders use art as a way to bend the truth of their *political* status. A cowardly leader might request to be painted with a menacing facade. A ruler in debt may demand to be surrounded by wealth in a painting. A self-consciously short king may have a tall statue of himself built in the center of town. A queen who hates the snot-nosed brats at a local orphanage may have a portrait made of her embracing them.

These are all important measures a monarch must take to control *perception*. So whatever you're lacking as a ruler, whether it be bravery, wealth, height, or compassion, make your portraits and statues show the opposite and no one will ever be the wiser.

Naturally, I wouldn't know about it personally. This is one of the many instances where my citizens are lucky to have a genuinely beautiful and brilliant queen. I don't think an artist could *improve* me if they tried. It's known throughout my kingdom that I'm much more beautiful than my paintings and sculptures imply.

There you have it: the Royal APP explained! If you practice it routinely, you will convince not only your people of your perfection, but also yourself!

It's a lot of pressure to put on one's shoulders, but to quote Queen Snow White's friends at the dwarf mines: "Pressure is what separates the dirt from the diamonds."

Only once you've perfected your image would I advise moving your attention to a secondary priority, like your kingdom and people's needs. Remember, there is no kingdom without the *I*.

Chapter 3

Be Cautious of Compliments

One of the first things they teach a new leader is to beware of flattery. Someone may be using praise and compliments as a way of gaining your trust, only to betray you in the end. You must guard your heart and keep a lookout for people with alternative motives.

While I'm sure this is a great lesson for *ugly people* in positions of power, I can safely say it doesn't apply to me. As you know, I'm overwhelmingly beautiful. If I distanced myself from every flatterer, I would have to live in total solitude. In fact, it's more concerning when someone is in my presence and they *don't* compliment me. *Those* are the people I need to keep an eye on.

Thankfully, I don't have to be suspicious of praise like some rulers do. Anyone who pays me a compliment is just stating a basic fact. To say I'm brilliant or beautiful is like saying the sun is bright or the grass is green. And *facts* have never influenced my decision making in the slightest.

Unfortunately, so many leaders must be cautious of compliments because they are not blessed with my attractiveness. It takes all the fun out of being a monarch, if you ask me. If a king or queen cannot enjoy someone basking in their glory from time to time, then what is the point of wearing a crown?

Thanks to my fortunate looks, I believe I've unintentionally come up with a solution for this matter. No matter how unattractive you are, *create a law that forces your people to compliment you!* Make everyone in your presence praise you at least three times an hour. Even compliment *yourself*—don't get out of bed until you've told yourself how wonderful you are! Drown yourself in praise so the harm-doers are muted. If *everyone* is praising you, the people plotting against you will have to find another way into your head. And if *everyone* is getting to you, *no one* can.

Sometimes the best way to prevent a burn is by lighting yourself on fire! (In one of his edits, Charlie has informed me I need to be very clear that this is a joke. Please do not treat burns with fire.)

Chapter 4

Appointing Royal Subjects

It's difficult to trust people when you're a monarch—that's why it's of grave importance to appoint people you can depend on into your circle of royal subjects. You mustn't be too hard on yourself if you discover one of them is plotting your downfall, as this is a common occurrence. The good news is, if a royal subject betrays or disappoints you, you can have them killed. That's why we rulers invented the wonderful term *treason*. It keeps everyone on their toes!

The person you appoint must be a good fit with the position you bestow. Whatever you assign someone to do, everyone in your kingdom must agree that they are the best person for the job. Luckily, since I established a new government, I was able to make up the titles as I went. For your reference, here is a list of my royal subjects and why I decided to appoint them to the position they hold.

The Third Little Pig, Chief of Staff

You need someone very responsible to spearhead all your political endeavors. They must come to the table already proven of wise decision making and the capability of handling stressful situations. I thought no one in the kingdom had done this better than the third Little Pig. He's famous for making good choices! His smart idea to build his home with bricks instead of other materials saved his life from the Big Bad Wolf. Since then, he's helped my reign with his meticulous organization skills and subtle advice when I'm faced with a hard choice myself. He's my rock—or *brick*, rather.

Lady Muffet, Secretary of Defense

After her famous encounter with a spider, Lady Muffet vowed that would be the last thing to "sit down beside her" without her consent. Lady Muffet manages the kingdom's defense exactly as she manages her own—by always keeping one eye open on the environment she's in and removing herself from all signs of danger. The poor thing is a curds-and-whey addict, but thankfully it hasn't interfered with her work.

Sir BaaBaa Blacksheep, Secretary of Treasury

Sir Blacksheep is the most optimistic animal I know, which is a very important quality for the lamb in charge of the kingdom's money. Just as he famously budgeted his wool, Sir Blacksheep always manages to keep us from falling into debt. Every time I ask him if the kingdom's financial state is positive, he replies, "Yes, ma'am, yes, ma'am. Three banks full." (Sir Henny Penny was my previous Secretary of Treasury, but he was too much of a worrywart. Government is no place for a nut who constantly thinks the sky is falling.)

Sir Jack Horner, Secretary of Nutrition

A fed kingdom is a happy kingdom, and Sir Jack Horner is a genius when it comes to handling our food supply. Even in the middle of a famine, he'll work tirelessly with farmers until they come up with enough food for everyone. He can stick his thumb into almost anything and pull out a plum. That reminds me, it's gotten a little inappropriate recently. . . . I really should talk to him about it.

Three Blind Mice, Supreme Court Justices

Justice is blind, and so are they! This was an easy decision to make. The Three Blind Mice never judge someone based on their race, gender, orientation, or background, but instead base their verdicts solely on the evidence brought to the court's attention. With that said, I'll admit they're a little harder on certain *species* than others—in particular, the feline population. It's resulted in the biggest cat emigration in history, but no one in the kingdom has really missed them.

The Little Old Woman from the Shoe Inn, Chief Historian

It's good to have a living history book on your side to remind you of all the mistakes your predecessors have made. I thought the Little Old Woman was the perfect person for the job. After raising a dozen children and hundreds of grandchildren, what *hasn't* she seen? It's a miracle her mind is in the condition it's in. It's remarkable how easily she can reference something from the past. Getting her to *shut up* about history has been tricky.

Granny, Chief Advisor

Last but certainly not least, my chief advisor could be no one else but my beloved granny. The chief advisor is the most important person to a monarch; you must trust them with your life, and they must have *your* best interests at heart. Granny is always good about doing the things I cannot before making a crucial decision, like *research*. I couldn't run my kingdom as successfully if it weren't for her. To be honest, I'm not sure Granny even realizes she has an official title—she may just be opinionated.

Chapter 5

Peasants Are Like Pets

Similar to creating your image, it is very important to establish a *relationship* with your people. On top of knowing *who* you are, it's good for them to know what *type* of ruler they're dealing with.

It's widely believed that there are only two options a leader can choose from: being a *tyrant* or a *caretaker*. As Nicole Macarena famously asks in her book *The Prince*, "Is it better to be *feared* or *loved*?" or something like that.

I'm paraphrasing, obviously. I'm running a kingdom and writing a book; there is no time to reference things.

This is a decision kings and queens struggle to make, for every monarch views his or her institution differently. Kings often choose the tyrant path. They command their kingdoms like captains on ships, barking orders and forcing respect by instilling fear. Usually, queens take a more maternal approach. They treat their people like their own children and hope for admiration in exchange for their compassion.

Personally, I don't see how either of these works. Too much fear could lead to resentment, while too much love could lead to vulnerability. It's not a question of "cruelty versus mercy" as Macarena suggests but finding the right balance of cruelty *and* mercy. So now I would like to make history by presenting a *third* option. Luckily for you, I have perfectly characterized what the ideal relationship between a ruler and their citizens should be!

Peasants Are Like Pets

Obviously I'm aware that comparing my people to animals kept on leashes will raise a few eyebrows, so allow me to defend this philosophy. Here are a few examples that will undoubtedly convince you:

1. Just like pets, peasants must be fed, given shelter, awarded when good and disciplined when bad, and cared for emotionally.

You can't possibly argue with that, so I'll continue.

2. Dominance must be established. Pets must always know you are in charge and that if they cross you they'll be punished. (Come to think of it, this is the basis of *all* my relationships.)

Are we still in agreement? Good!

3. If your pet gets into a neighbor's yard, you become responsible for whatever damage is done. And if they bite someone, you'll have to put them down.

I'll explain further: If one of my citizens went into a neighboring kingdom and caused harm, it would reflect poorly on *me*—especially if I did nothing about it. A war might break out if rulers didn't distance themselves from crimes committed by their people.

Just last week, Queen Rapunzel sent an arsonist from her kingdom to the gallows for trying to set an estate in the Charming Kingdom ablaze. She had no choice— if she didn't take action, the Charming family would have been offended. (I even heard the noose was made of Rapunzel's hair, but that sounds a little too desperate—even for Rapunzel.)

In short, keep an eye on your citizens. The wall around my kingdom wasn't built only to keep the wolves out; it's also to keep the troublemaking idiots inside. Shall I proceed?

4. You must entertain your pets. A restless pet is more likely to lash out at their master than a well-exercised one is.

This is why it's very important to create traditions and celebrations for your people to participate in. Throw a parade, host a ceremony, give them a holiday once in a while! Make your people feel good about being your citizens so they never gang together and plot your downfall. Make sense? Terrific!

5. You must be very clear with your pets about what is and isn't acceptable behavior:
A) They must be shown the proper places to use the restroom. B) Guests are not to be jumped on. C) They must be taught that chewing, barking, and humping your leg will not be tolerated.

I wish the traits mentioned above applied only to pets, but we have our fair share of bizarre people in this kingdom—it's a long story. *Moving on!* Last but not least:

6. In moments of weakness, you can distract your pets with shiny objects.

If there is any confusion regarding how this applies to peasants, please see the part about jewelry in chapter 2.

As I've brilliantly laid out, it's not about being feared or loved but how you define a combination of the two. In my opinion, imagining yourself as the caring but authoritative master of a doe-eyed helpless creature is the most effective way to run a kingdom. Am I good, or am I good?

If you're timid about this philosophy, I recommend adopting a pet. I've learned more about governing from my overgrown canine, Clawdius, than from all the current and previous rulers in history.

However you decide to label your relationship with your people, it's very crucial you do it quickly. The earlier you set guidelines and boundaries, the sooner they'll adapt and grow accustomed to them.

You NEVER want to surprise your people! A *surprising* monarch may come across as an *irrational* one; irrationality leads to hatred, and hatred leads to a revolution, and a revolution leads to dirty villagers running amok in your castle. And if there's one thing I hate more than anything, it's uninvited guests.

A ruler must be pleasantly predictable at all times, yet also exercise spontaneity when it's safe. There's a thin line between predictability and repetition, and being repetitive could lead to disappointment. In that regard, reigning is like cooking a lamb stew: Only spice things up when you're certain it won't result in heartburn or indigestion. No one wants to live in a gassy monarchy.

❁

Well, I've used a lot of big words and clever metaphors in this chapter. I'm very proud of myself. Being a political genius is exhausting, so I think I'll put my quill down and call it a night.

I have to get up early tomorrow and *walk my kingdom!* Get it? *Because peasants are like pets.* . . . Yes, good night.

Chapter 6

✦✦✦

Making a Scandal Work for You

Nothing can damage a monarch's reputation like a scandal. Your enemies will constantly be on the lookout for something they can use to tarnish your name, whether it's political or personal. Since a scandal is bound to surface during your reign, I wouldn't waste your time trying to prevent the inevitable—that would be *exhausting*! Instead, save your energy for when a scandal presents itself and then put all your effort into *making the scandal work for you!*

A couple years ago, I was on the brink of a humiliation that almost cost me the throne. Luckily, I brilliantly spun the situation to work in my favor and make my criticizers look like terrible and heartless people. Remember, when someone points a finger at you, they point three at themselves (unless they have hooves; then ignore this expression).

You must develop a talent for finding what your enemies' opposing fingers are pointing at! Anyone willing to openly criticize you will undoubtedly have something for you to criticize back! I'll explain....

One afternoon, I treated my royal subjects to a delightful lunch at the castle. Everyone was there—Granny, the Little Old Woman from the Shoe Inn, the third Little Pig, Sir Jack Horner, Lady Muffet, and Sir BaaBaa Blacksheep. But the Three Blind Mice showed up late because their nephew, Hickory Dickory, had gotten into some trouble with a clock again. (Where is Puss in Boots when you need him?)

We were having a wonderful time gossiping about notable people in the kingdom. We laughed over our suspicions of what really happened between Jack and Jill on the hill, if Humpty Dumpty's widow had anything to do with his death, and if Georgie Porgie's current relationship would outlast the previous disasters—the usual topics.

Suddenly, the Little Old Woman blurted out, "Did you hear the chatter about *Queen Red*?"

The poor dear is hard of hearing and has gone senile in recent years (I probably would, too, if I lived in a boot with 150 grandchildren). She had obviously forgotten she was in my presence. Other monarchs may have taken offense to this, but it's actually the reason I keep the Little Old Woman around. If you want *unbiased social insight*, I recommend befriending an absentminded old lady with nothing to prove.

"Can't say I have," I said through a pained smile. *"Please share."*

The other subjects were mortified. They gestured for her to be quiet, but the Little Old Woman thought they were just eager to hear.

"The rumor in our sewing group is that she's shacking up with a large amphibian!" she said with excited eyes. "It's a *cross-species catastrophe*!"

I turned pale and my chest felt very tight (my corset didn't help). I was shocked, not because it was an outrageous lie but because it was *true*—I just had never thought of it that way! The public is excellent at making things seem as bad as possible.

"You mean *Charlie*?" I said. "But he isn't *just* a frog—he's a prince on the inside!"

My subjects batted their eyes pityingly at me. The third Little Pig patted my shoulder sympathetically.

"Love is in the eye of the beholder," he said.

"No, I mean he's LITERALLY a prince!" I said. *"He was cursed to look like a frog by a witch when he was young! I would never be interested unless I knew there was a royal somewhere inside him!"*

"Well, I suppose it's what's inside that counts," Granny said.

Regardless, this was terrible news! If the kingdom elders were talking about it as they crocheted tea cozies, the *rest* of the kingdom was surely talking about it, too! It would only be a matter of time before my relationship with Charlie was deemed *unnatural* or *demonic* and I would be labeled a *freak* and *unfit to lead*! I had to do something drastic. And I had to do it *fast!*

The next day I called the entire kingdom to the castle. I stepped out onto the balcony and announced the following to the crowd below:

"Fellow Hoodians, because of your adorable obsession with me, I trust you've all heard the rumor about my relationship with the frog man. At this time, I feel I must tell you that this rumor . . . *is absolutely true!*"

A collective gasp swept through the crowd. I tend to be dramatic when addressing my people, but it's very important to entertain them. The more stimulating you are, the more people show up when you summon them.

"I recently heard our relationship referred to as a *cross-species catastrophe!* This was very troubling, and it concerned me so much I lost twenty minutes of sleep last night. You see, this frog man is an amphibian only on the outside. *Inside*, he's the long-lost Charming prince who was *cursed* to look like a frog many years ago. I've chosen to love him despite his flaws, just as I love you."

(Do you see what I did there? I replaced their mistrust with sympathy! *Goooooo, Queen Red!*)

"Even though people have spread word of our relationship in an attempt to hurt me, I already forgive you for believing it. It takes a person of impeccable judgment to look past a person's appearance, so I would never expect you to see him as I do."

(When you can, guilt people into loving you! It's as effective as it is fun.)

"However, what troubled me the most was not that it was characterized as a *cross-species* relationship, but that everyone's immediate reaction was to shun it as an offense against nature. *Are we still living in the Dragon Age?* I would hope by now we're sophisticated enough to realize love is love, regardless of age, color, gender, and yes, *species*. That is why I would like to publically declare that, as long as I am your queen, everyone in my kingdom will have the right to love whomever they wish!"

The declaration was met with an enthusiastic round of applause. I even had to clap for myself—I turned a scandal conspired against me into something my people could respect and admire me more for. *I'd like to see Cinderella top that!*

A farmer in the front of the crowd raised his hand.

"Yes, noble farmer?" I asked. "What is your question?"

"Does this mean I can marry my cow?" he asked.

I definitely wasn't expecting this.

"That depends," I said. "Does your cow love you as much as you love it? Do you miss each other when you're apart? Does your cow embody your happiness? Do you look into each other's eyes and know you've found your other half?"

The farmer shook his head. "No, she just eats grass all day."

"Does she even talk?" I asked.

"No," he said. "She's a simple cow."

At this point, I couldn't hide my annoyance. "Then *no!* You can't marry your cow. And you're ridiculous for asking."

"Your Majesty?" a woman asked. "Then what's the difference between loving a cow and loving the frog man?"

"Seriously, people?" I asked. "Do I really need to spell this out for you?"

Judging by the blank doe-eyed expressions on the dirty faces throughout the crowd, I *did*.

"There is a major difference between an animal who can communicate and reason, and one who grazes all day," I said. "No one should marry anything they can't share a conversation or a mutual hobby with." .

"But what if *I* liked to eat grass all day, too?" the farmer asked. "Are we allowed to love each other if there are similar interests?"

It was one of the first times I wanted to take off my tiara and throw it at someone. Now do you see why *I'm* the queen?

"As long as both parties can definitively express their happiness and desire to be with the other, *fantastic!* Otherwise, *no!* Those are the best guidelines I can give you."

"Fair enough," the farmer said, and the rest of the crowd nodded along with him.

"Would you recommend being in a cross-species relationship?" the woman asked. "Like, if I haven't found the right human yet, should I broaden my search?"

"I'm not saying one is better than the other," I specified. "I'm just saying we should all have an open mind when it comes to love. You'll never really know what you're looking for until you find it. Trust me, I spent years pursuing the man I thought was *the love of my life.* He was the closest thing to perfection I had ever known, besides myself, so I was certain we were meant for each other. Thankfully, I learned I was wrong before it was too late. I found true happiness with someone who was the opposite of what I was looking for. He's not the definition of perfection, but he's perfect to me."

"Are you talking about Jack?" the farmer said. "Is he the man you pursued?"

"Of course she's talking about Jack!" another woman said. "Everyone knows she was madly in love with Jack!"

"Hold on a second!" I yelled. "*Everyone* knew that?"

The crowd nodded in unison.

"Didn't Jack choose an outlaw over you, Your Majesty?" a child asked. "At least, that's what all the children at school say."

My face suddenly felt very warm and my jewelry felt extra heavy.

"Well, I think that's enough groundbreaking history for one afternoon. Now, I must be alone to think about matters of the kingdom. *Enjoy the rest of your day!*"

There you have it: a travesty avoided! I masterfully went to the root of the issue and turned a weed into a beautiful flower! Not to mention making history in the process—and all before afternoon tea! I sure pity the monarchs who will succeed me; no one will be able to hold a candle to my reign!

The Snow Queen

The Evil Queen

The Giant

The Wicked Stepmother

Ezmia, The Enchantress

The Sea Witch

Chapter 7

Avoiding Hatred and Villainy

Nothing in politics is black and white, but we do live in a world obsessed with labeling people as *heroes* or *villains*. Any leader who falls into a "gray area" is rarely remembered. In fact, I can't think of a single leader in history who was just *decent*. My tutors must have skipped the lessons about *Anne the Ample*, *Stephen the Simple*, and *Mary the Mediocre*.

Unfortunately, *great* or *terrible* are the only options if you want to make a splash. It's a slippery slope to Herotown, and all the shortcuts usually lead to Villainville, so never rush your reputation. Remember, every reign has bumps in the road, so don't panic if you go through a "disliked" phase. This phase will turn into a legacy only if you grow impatient. Citizens always see through their leaders' pathetic attempts to regain respect. (Except for my citizens—it usually goes right over their heads. *Lucky me!*)

In my opinion, being classified as a villain is just the result of a mishandled scandal. (Fortunately, I've already taught you how to manage that in the previous chapter.) Despite popular belief within my kingdom, we can actually learn from other people's mistakes! So rather than distancing yourself from someone's downfall, I recommend putting yourself in their shoes (even the ugly pairs).

By evaluating how some of the poorest saps in history conducted a situation, we can learn how to productively assess our own rough patches in the future. Besides, it's just fun to judge people!

The Evil Queen

Snow White's stepmother is remembered for lounging around her luxurious palace and staring into mirrors all day. I do the exact same thing, so why am I so beloved, while the Evil Queen is not? It's because I let my people know *why* I do it (please see chapter 2).

The Evil Queen didn't care what her people thought, so they drew their own conclusions and she never recovered. Ultimately, I think the Evil Queen's *lack of communication* and *inability to think things through* led to her downfall.

Here's what I think she should have done differently:

1. The Evil Queen should have been honest from the beginning about her past. By the time the truth came out (her boyfriend was imprisoned in a mirror *blah blah blah*...she was only vain so he didn't forget her *blah blah blah*...she

had a heart of stone *cue the violin* ...), it was too late! People's opinion of her was already sealed! Had people known the truth, she would have her own holiday right now, not be trapped at the bottom of a dump. (It's a long story, so if you have questions, ask a friend.)

2. I'm not promoting violence, but the Evil Queen could have come up with easier ways to kill Snow White. For instance, they lived in a HUGE palace with lots of stairs and windows. Had Snow White just "accidently tripped down steps" or "fallen out a window," no one would have suspected foul play! Also, Snow White was so pale she was practically see-through. Had the Evil Queen just locked her outside during a blizzard, no one would have found her until spring!

3. When the Evil Queen was accused of killing Snow White, she had the opportunity to come up with a great defense. For example, "Wait

a second. You're telling me my stepdaughter ran away from home, shacked up with seven strange men for a few months, and now she's accusing me of trying to kill her with *a poisoned apple?* And you think *I'm* the imbalanced one?'"

We can learn three things from the Evil Queen: Always be honest so you aren't misunderstood, do your dirty work behind closed doors, and if you're not smart enough to devise a good alibi, don't commit a crime!

The Wicked Stepmother

In retrospect, Cinderella's stepmother makes Snow White's stepmother look like *mother of the year.* I've never understood why people dislike her so much. I mean, many stepparents don't get along with their stepchildren. Had I been Cinderella's stepmother, I would have stated one of the following in my defense when the kingdom turned on me.

1. "Yes, I gave Cinderella chores to do around the house. Just like every parent *ever*." (For the record, if your child is obviously common, like Cinderella, I support the assignment of chores. I only have a problem with it when the child shows a higher level of potential, such as I did.)

2. "I didn't want Cinderella to go to the ball, because *Cinderella talks to mice*. Would *you* let that kind of crazy out of the house?"

3. "I can't be much worse than her real mother. Cinderella's mother named her after *dirt*."

4. "Of course I tried tricking the prince into marrying my daughters. Have you met my daughters? They're awful. Would *you* want to be stuck with them for the rest of your life?"

5. "Obviously I never wanted Cinderella to be queen. Cinderella wore glass shoes to a dance party. Do you consider that leadership material?"

Clearly, the Wicked Stepmother had many logical points with which to defend herself. Instead, she stayed quiet and sequestered herself from the kingdom, only making herself look guiltier. This teaches us that *the right to remain silent* isn't always the *right move*.

The Sea Witch

Proof we can learn something from all of God's creatures—even a foul-smelling sea-lice-covered crustacean can teach us something. The Sea Witch has a unique status; she's considered a villain even though she's never really committed a crime. She never *forced* anyone to make a trade with her; the Little Mermaid willingly sought her out to make a trade. It's the morbid way the Sea Witch goes about her business that gives her such a villainous reputation.

> Example 1: In exchange for legs, the Sea Witch
> cut the Little Mermaid's tongue out of her mouth.
> *What is wrong with this woman? What does she*

possibly need a tongue for? Would a nice shell not have been sufficient?

Example 2: When the Little Mermaid decided to be a mermaid again, the Sea Witch traded a magic dagger in exchange for her sisters' *hair*! (Makes me glad to be an only child!) She then instructed the Little Mermaid to stab the man she loved in the heart to reverse the spell. *Um . . . gross! Was this REALLY necessary?*

I've had the misfortune of meeting the Sea Witch—what she really should be trading for is some scented candles! Which brings me to:

Example 3: Her home is decorated in dead body parts! She uses a whale's rib cage as a staircase! *Would it kill her to have nice floral wallpaper or a few accent pillows?* People will judge you on how you choose to present yourself. If you have macabre tastes, save them for behind closed doors.

Overall, the Sea Witch is *disgusting and complicated for sport.* She enjoys being grotesque and difficult, which is very unnecessary. If you're blessed to have the upper hand in a situation, don't choose to slap people with it. They might slap you back on your way down.

The Snow Queen

The Snow Queen is the ultimate *ice queen*. I don't care how cold your lifestyle is—no one has an excuse to be as bitter as she is.

The Snow Queen was once the most feared weather witch throughout the kingdoms. She used to rule the north until Snow White's father reclaimed it and founded the Northern Kingdom. Since then, she spends her days pouting in isolation and sends violent blizzards through the Northern Mountains whenever she wakes up on the wrong side of the bed. She was also so upset about losing power that her eyes froze with tears and then melted away!

How pathetic is that? The lesson here is to *handle your defeats with dignity*. No one is going to respect or admire a gloomy and jaded old queen.

The Giant

Tantrums make everyone look small, especially giants. I understand why the Giant was angry. Jack snuck into his home, stole some money, and rescued the enchanted (and terribly annoying) harp. The Giant felt belittled.

However, if the Giant had just taken a deep breath and counted to ten, rather than chased a boy one-sixteenth his size down a beanstalk in a rage, he would still be alive today! Like my granny always says: "Don't get mad—get even!" When retaliating, make sure you're practicing *intelligent revenge* so you don't overreact and cause yourself more harm.

The Giant's downfall (literally a *downfall!*) teaches us to *have some self-respect* and not to *sweat over the small stuff.* Which I suppose is everything when you're a giant....(Fun fact: *We also learned giant carcasses make excellent fertilizer!*)

Ezmia the Enchantress

Now, here's a villain for the ages! This fairy gone rogue redefined the word *selfish*! All the royal families including myself were dragged for miles by vines because of her! I refuse to defend her, so I'll dive right into my evaluation.

Ezmia's biggest problem was that she had absolutely everything she needed: power, beauty, intelligence, and an adorable sidekick—yet she still wanted more! She was a colossal brat and as shallow as an ant's teakettle! Her soul was like a bottomless pit that could never be filled. Being spoiled and greedy is a dangerous combination! Not all of us can manage it as well as I do.

Her ego was out of control! It blinded her judgment, making her vulnerable in ways she didn't think were possible. In the end, a couple snarky comments from a teenage girl were what defeated her. I saw it happen! Sticks and stones didn't break her bones; it was *words* that hurt her!

Almost the opposite of the Snow Queen, the Enchantress is a good example of someone who let their *success* get to their head! It made her careless and opened her up to weakness. Believing you are too big to fail will only result in failure!

Well, this has been a delightful chapter to write! Dissecting the flaws of famous people is one of my favorite hobbies. If only this book had been published earlier, history's most hated figures might have been remembered differently.

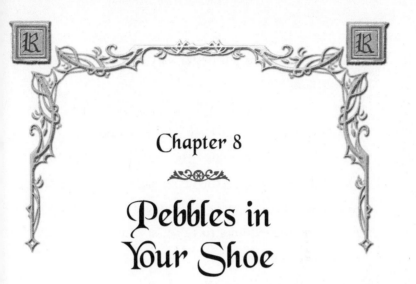

Chapter 8

Pebbles in Your Shoe

S ince this is our eighth chapter together, I'm going to tell you a little secret: I despise orphans. I mean, what good are they? When is the last time an orphan asked you how *your* day was? Can you name one "exceptional orphan" you've met?

I just read the previous paragraph aloud to Charlie and his mouth dropped open. He's informed me I need to explain myself better so I don't come across as heartless.

The "orphans" in the Red Riding Hood Kingdom did not lose their parents—they're all alive and well. The children living in the orphanages are the bratty, mischievous, and greedy delinquents who were too much for their parents to raise, so they became the government's problem.

This was entirely my fault and I take full responsibility. When I first opened the orphanages, there was a minor miscommunication with the scribe I was dictating my plans to. I said the orphanages were for "the children of *deceased* parents," but that idiot wrote down "children of *distressed* parents." I should have made him read it back to me, but I had scheduled an important nap to take afterward. By the time the typo came to my attention, the decree had already been posted all over the country. The next thing I knew, mothers and fathers from all corners of the kingdom had dragged their rambunctious children into town and left them on my doorstep.

Since then, those terrors have caused us nothing but headaches! They're constantly sneaking out at night to play pranks around the kingdom! They put soap in the Little Boy Who Cried Wolf Memorial Fountain. They stained the wool on Little Bo Peep's sheep, causing a tie-dyed-coat trend that winter. They've locked cats inside henhouses, glued cows' hooves to the ground, and even filled Lady Muffet's mailbox with spiders. The list goes on!

However, despite loathing them, I can never let my detestation show. It's very important a monarch never reveal a *pebble* in their shoe, for their enemies may turn it into a *boulder!*

So, to keep up appearances, I spend one day every year with the orphans to disguise my disgust. During which the orphans and I play games like "tie the queen up," "tiara Frisbee," "guess what's under her dress," "Will she sink or swim?" and my favorite, "Is that a wig?" The kingdom thinks I'm being generous, the orphans think I like them, and no one is the wiser.

The only thing that gets me through the day is know-ing that when they become adults, I'll get to tar and feather them. This visual has saved me from losing my temper on several occasions when I'm forced to be with people who annoy me.

Chapter 9

Hosting Other Royals

If there's one thing I enjoy, it's a good party! I'm always looking for an excuse to throw one. Whenever one of my friends or relatives has a birthday or celebrates a special occasion, I put together a huge extravaganza in their honor. And sometimes they even attend!

Having a party on the horizon is a great way to get through a difficult situation. Every time I get kidnapped or narrowly escape death (which happens so often you'd think they were my hobbies), I plan a special event in my head. Just knowing you'll be surrounded by friends, music, games, food, drinks, and matching furniture can bring a little sunshine to the cloudiest days.

This trick was tremendously helpful when the Enchantress kidnapped me. There I was, strapped to a wall by enchanted vines with all the other royals. The fear of death wasn't even the worst part; we had to suffer through hours of a repetitive soliloquy as the Enchantress bragged about her universal domination—it's a wonder our ears didn't bleed!

As I looked around at all the gloomy faces, a little voice in my head whispered, *"Wouldn't it be fun to have an 'I survived the Enchantress' party when this mess is over?"* Instantly my frown was turned upside down and the party-planning gears in my head rotated at full speed. I was so excited I almost forgot I had been kidnapped at all.

What kind of party did I want it to be? Being held prisoner always gives me an appetite, so I figured a dinner party would be the most fun to think about. *Where did*

I want to have the party? I had just remodeled my castle, so naturally I wanted to show it off. *Who was I going to invite?* All the captive royals around me looked like they could use a party. I figured it might be nice to spend time together by *choice* for a change. Maybe it would make the next time we were imprisoned together more enjoyable.

With my plans in motion, I began passing out verbal invitations while the Enchantress was on another tangent of self-congratulations.

"Pssssst, Snow White," I whispered. *"Snow White, over here!"*

Snow White was a little wrapped up in the situation, so it took a while to get her attention. *"What is it, Red?"* she whispered back.

"I want to invite you and Chandler to my castle for dinner!" I said, and gave her a thumbs-up.

"Um...sounds nice...," Snow White said. She wasn't as enthusiastic as I'd hoped, but I couldn't blame her

given what we were going through at the time. Not everyone knows how to handle a crisis as well as I do.

"Hey, Sleeping Beauty!" I whispered, but she was either too far to hear or just ignoring me. *"If you can hear me, you and Chase are invited to my castle for dinner once this ordeal is over!"*

"Red, what are you doing?!" Rapunzel whispered to me.

"I'm inviting everyone to my castle for a party," I said.

"The Enchantress is about to kill us! We're not going to have a party!" Rapunzel snipped.

"Not with that attitude," I said. *"You're not invited if you're going to be such a downer!"*

Rapunzel was probably just upset I hadn't asked her first. I turned my head to Goldilocks and Jack, who were pinned to the wall next to me.

"Goldilocks, you and Jack should come to—"

"We already have plans," Goldilocks said before I could finish. Typical! You'd think a fugitive would be more fun.

While I've never been the biggest fan of Cinderella's, it would have been rude not to include her, since I was inviting everyone else.

"Cinderella!" I said, and we made eye contact. *"This probably isn't the best time, but I'm going to host a dinner at my castle. I would love to have you and Chance come if you're not busy. No children, though, so get a sitter for Hope—sorry about her getting kidnapped, by the way! Worst week ever, am I right?"*

"Uh-huh," she mumbled.

In the end, everyone had panicked for no reason. The Enchantress was defeated, we were all freed, and life returned to normal.

The Enchantress taking over the world was *nothing* compared to the stress of planning the party! I'd never realized how much pressure comes with hosting a party for royals until I got into the thick of things! I regretted inviting them the minute I started making plans. But to no surprise, I rose to the occasion and planned a lovely and successful evening!

Here are some recommendations should you ever host one yourself—especially if I'm invited.

Impressing from the Start

Remember, unlike your friends and relatives, royal families are accustomed to exquisite things. It's almost impossible to impress them! So here's my method of planning: Picture an evening from start to finish filled with things that would impress you—*now double that expectation!* Now take that image and add as many shiny objects as you can visualize without having a seizure. That will *still* underwhelm them, but stop there. Anything more than that will seem tacky.

I was worried they might have forgotten about my party after that whole "end of the world" thing we survived. So I sent two dozen horn players and a minstrel to each of their palaces to perform a musical invitation as a subtle reminder.

It took me two weeks of meticulous planning to make our evening a spectacular event to remember. The dining room was decorated in gold tablecloths and gold candlesticks. I had twelve of my favorite portraits of me hung so we would have something pleasant to look at while we ate. I also had all the floors recarpeted, all the art cleaned, and all the furniture reupholstered in the other rooms just in case someone wanted a tour.

Not only did the castle have to look its best, but also the kingdom needed to look better than ever. I traveled around the kingdom and ordered my people to clean up their yards, paint their barns, and keep their unattractive family members indoors. On the day of the dinner, I made my citizens line the streets in their best clothes—bonnets and bowties, I said. They smiled and waved at the royals as they entered our kingdom and traveled to my castle.

I waited on the landing of the grand staircase in the entrance hall, dressed in my best gown, hood, gloves, and jewels, and greeted each of the monarchs as they arrived. It's important to be playful when welcoming other heads of state. There's nothing worse than hosting a stiff dinner.

"*Cinderella*, you look wonderful! Who says you need a Fairy Godmother's help to put a look together?!" "*Sleeping Beauty*, my, how rested you look! I wish someone would curse me to sleep for one hundred years!" "Darling *Rapunzel*, I love what you've done with your hair! Is the rest of it still making its way out of your carriage?" "Oh my, *Snow White*! Are you all right? It looks like you've seen a ghost!"

Snow White looked at me oddly and then finally sighed. "Oh, it's a joke...because I'm so pale...*Funny*."

"I hope you all had pleasant journeys! How do you all like my kingdom?" I asked.

"It's . . . *cute*," Cinderella said. "Do your people always line the streets and wave at your guests?"

"Were they doing that again? Oh, those silly dears. I told them it wasn't necessary! They just love welcoming people to their beautiful home."

"I wouldn't say it was *welcoming*," Sleeping Beauty said. "It was a little unsettling, actually, like something in a nightmare. I was afraid they were going to attack our carriage."

All the royals nodded along with concerned eyes. Perhaps the citizens were a bit much.

"Well, with the amount of time you've slept, I'm sure everything reminds you of a nightmare." I laughed awkwardly. *"Who's hungry?"*

Making Special Accommodations

Royals like feeling special (it's in our genes), so it's your job to make them feel special while they're in your home. This can be challenging when hosting multiple guests who wear crowns. Don't worry, it doesn't have to be an obnoxious display of affection (although one wouldn't hurt if I'm in your home). All we need is a little something to show that you put our personal needs into consideration.

For example, as I escorted my guests to the dining room, I made a point to show Cinderella where all the exits were.

"Why are you showing me these?" Cinderella asked. "Do you want me to leave?"

"Of course not!" I said. "It's just in case you need to make a mad dash at midnight. We all know you're usually the first one out the door."

"That's *kind* of you," she said, "but I'm not planning to leave earlier than anyone else. The Fairy Godmother is watching Princess Hope tonight, so there's no curfew! I'll happily sit at your side until the evening comes to an end."

"Oh, you were planning to sit with us?" I said. "I had them set a special place for you with the servants downstairs. I figured you'd be more comfortable given your history of service."

Judging by her face, this was more kindness than she was willing to accept. I assured her it would be no trouble to have them set an extra place in the dining room. I think I gained major points with Cinderella that night. We might even be considered *friends* now! It's amazing what a little hospitality can do.

Before the appetizer was served, while Charlie was entertaining the men and Granny was showing the women my portraits, I pulled Snow White aside.

"Just to let you know, I made sure tonight's meal would be entirely apple-free," I said with an adorable wink. "I didn't want you to be worried about dietary restrictions tonight."

"Oh, thank you," Snow White said. "But just so you know, I'm not *allergic* to apples. The one my stepmother tried to kill me with was *poisoned*—it could have harmed anyone. I actually like apples."

"Ah," I said. "That's what I meant. I told my chef, 'absolutely no poisoned apples tonight!' We'll send those to the orphanage."

Snow White never laughs at my jokes. I have a feeling my humor is above her comprehension, the poor thing. I even had the chef bring out an apple with a small sign that read NOT POISONED. She didn't laugh at that, either.

Roughly halfway through the first course, Sleeping Beauty gently tapped me on the shoulder.

"Red, out of curiosity, why is there a pillow next to my place setting?" she asked.

"I had that placed there in case you needed to take a rest," I explained. "Don't worry, I won't be offended in the slightest. I can't imagine how the curse affected your sleep cycle."

"Thank you, but I won't be needing it," she said defensively. "Now that my kingdom has been restored and the Enchantress is gone for good, I've been sleeping quite regularly."

The poor thing must have been in denial about it. Later in the evening, during one of my longer toasts, I caught her dozing off for a bit. (Now that I mention it, Granny and Charlie had fallen asleep, too. There must have been something in the soup.)

Conversation

A gathering is only as good as the chemistry between its guests. It's wise to come up with a list of topics beforehand to keep your company stimulated. I wanted to discuss intelligent matters that would spark everyone's interest. Dinner conversation isn't fun unless everyone can partake and enjoy it. So this is the list I came up with, which you may use as a template:

    1. How has Queen Red influenced you the most?

2. What is something about the Red Riding Hood Kingdom you wish you could do with yours?

3. Which of Queen Red's dresses is your favorite?

4. Why is *your* Prince Charming the most charming?

5. How has Queen Red recently impressed you?

6. If my prince hadn't rescued me, I would probably be _____ right now.

7. Which great leader, living or dead, does Queen Red remind you of?

8. Mermaids: Fish or Mammals?

9. If you had Rapunzel's hair, what's the craziest thing you'd do with it?

10. Damsels in distress: Are cries for help really just cries for attention?

11. What's one of Queen Red's qualities you wish you had more of?

12. Describe your ideal happily-ever-after.

Be Prepared for the Worst

Usually, the more important an occasion is, the more likely something will go terribly wrong. That's just the way it is. So if you're going to host a dinner for royalty, you need to be prepared for *ANYTHING*.

As you plan your event, carefully assess everything that could go wrong. By the time my guests arrived, there wasn't a single disruption I hadn't planned for.

- Although Snow White wasn't on the throne during the C.R.A.W.L. Revolution, I didn't want any hard feelings to surface between us. So, every time Granny brought up "the war against the north" (which is quite a bit when she gets around new people), I instructed a server to interrupt her with the next course.

- Unbeknownst to my guests, my pockets were full of bones to toss at Clawdius in case he got into trouble. The closest call was when I caught him chewing on Rapunzel's hair under the table. Luckily she didn't notice the large chunk he had eaten. (That couldn't have been easy to digest!)

- A butler was standing in the hall with a bucket of water during the entire meal should anything or anyone catch on fire. After my first castle burned down, I learned I had *flammable* taste.

- The knights' armor that decorated the corners of the dining room actually had soldiers inside them should a war or a revolution break out before dessert.

- I had the chef prepare an extra plate if someone brought an unexpected guest without telling me. My hunch proved to be right, because as the main course was being served, Cinderella found one of her pet mice had snuck into her pocket before leaving the Charming Palace. A normal person would think the dinner table was an inappropriate place for a rat—*not Cinderella!* She requested the extra plate and the rodent ate an entire rack of lamb by itself. Apparently, you can take the girl out of service, but you can't take the service out of the girl.

- I even had exit routes planned in the event of a natural disaster. There was no earthquake, flood, fire, or famine that was going to rain on my parade!

All in all, thanks to my extraordinary coordinating skills, the dinner was a huge success! There wasn't a single hitch! Each king and queen left much happier than they arrived and we made a plan to make plans of doing it again at someone else's palace.

I haven't heard from any of them, but that doesn't dishearten me. Obviously, my dinner was such a smash, they were all too intimidated to follow it! You know, if this queen thing doesn't work out, I think I have a great backup career. Perhaps *Queen Red Riding Hood's Guide to Event Planning* should have been my first book.

Chapter 10

Recommended Reading

S ince reading this book is probably the first time most of your brains have been so stimulated, I thought it would be kind to provide a list of titles I highly recommend reading after you conclude my book. It's very important to continue your "mush into matter" effort beyond this publication. Don't worry, I've summarized each book on your behalf and pointed out what you should learn from them.

Reading comprehension takes a lot of energy, so don't overdo it and pull a thinking muscle.

Queen Red Riding Hood's Guide to Royalty by **Queen Red Riding Hood**—Don't flip the book over to double-check the title—*this is in your hands!* I added my own book to this list for three reasons. Number one: It's by far the best political book out there—trust me, I've read most of them. Number two: It'll benefit you greatly to reread it in case you missed anything the first time around. Number three: Doesn't it make you feel accomplished knowing you've taken a step in the right direction?

The Prince by **Nicole Macarena**—This is the book that started it all! If you're curious to see what inspired my masterpiece, definitely check this out! I must warn you, it's not as delightful as my book and it's hard to read. To be honest, I didn't know what she was talking about most of the time. However, it won't be hard to recognize the ideas that I've so brilliantly updated. NOTE: When she talks about "principles," she isn't referring to the head of a school. I learned that the hard way.

Hamlet **by William Shakyfruit**—This selection is purely selfish because it's one of my favorite stories. To put it simply, it's absolutely hysterical. I mean, *everyone is royal, but they're all miserable!* Isn't that so amusing? And as punishment for their ridiculousness, they have obscene and theatrical deaths. There is a lot of political wisdom hidden throughout the silly plot, so much so that you forget it's a comedy at times. *Hamlet* is a script, so it can be a group activity if you'd like. I make my royal subjects come to the castle every Thursday afternoon and perform it for me.

Utopia **by Sir Thomas More**—Make sure you have a handkerchief handy, because this one is a tearjerker. It takes place on a miserable island where *everyone is treated the exact same—even the rulers!* It really makes you respect the monarchy and understand the importance of a class system. *Utopia* cleverly displays how too much equality can be a very dull thing.

The Mother Goose Diaries **by Mother Goose**—Remember that lesson about learning from other people's mistakes? This book proves that more than anything I've ever encountered. While I love Mother Goose dearly, much can be learned as you read about her interactions with rulers throughout history. Never take advice from an old woman who uses an overgrown farm animal as transportation. I thought that was a given, but I was wrong.

Outroduction

A Few Final Words

Unfortunately, all good things must come to an end, and I'm afraid this book is no exception. This may be the only time you'll come in contact with such profound wisdom, so do not be surprised if you experience a period of mourning and/or depression upon finishing it. But before you dive into the depths of withdrawal, let's celebrate the time we shared by reviewing what I've taught you:

You learned the extent of my bravery and brilliance as I told you my heroic tale, and hopefully it inspired you to be courageous in your own life.

I taught you the importance of image and the proper methods of gaining and maintaining respect and admiration from your people.

You were warned to be cautious of flattery, for it may be laced with deception.

I told you how to carefully choose the people who work for you and to appoint only people who are perfect for the position.

I explained that the ideal relationship between a monarch and his or her citizens resembles that between man and man's best friend.

When your enemies drag your name through the dirt, you can emerge covered in roses if you look for the flowers hidden in the field.

I showed you how learning from other people's mistakes is just as important as learning from their achievements if you want a successful reputation.

I taught you that if you keep your annoyances close to your heart, you can use them as a shield.

You learned the necessary steps of planning for and hosting important figures, which will lead to prosperous relationships with your neighbors.

I've given you a list of literature I recommend so you may continue your education of politics and royalty.

Finally, I will leave you with the best piece of advice I've ever been given, and the source will surprise you. Cinderella once told me, "Remember, Red, it's impossible to please everyone, so never make that a goal."

I'm embarrassed to admit I actually agree with the rat whisperer. But if there's one thing I've learned from my own balance of power and politics, of success and failure, of approval and disapproval, of luxury and responsibility, it's this: *You can't please everyone, so make sure you please yourself!*

Acknowledgments

So many people to thank, such little time! I would like to thank Charlie and Granny for editing my book and changing all the words I made up. To my darling Clawdius—*Mommy loves you!* A special thank-you to my friends Alex and Conner, whom I would love to see in an environment free of danger just once.

To all the wonderful people in my kingdom, I couldn't be queen without you—literally! A big thanks to my royal subjects: the third Little Pig, Lady Muffet, Sir Jack Horner, Sir BaaBaa Blacksheep, the Little Old Woman from the Shoe Inn, and the Three Blind

Mice. Thank you for looking after the kingdom so I could write about looking after the kingdom. Also, thank you for letting me pass the law to make buying a copy of this book mandatory to everyone in the kingdom—that will definitely help with sales!

I suppose some thanks should be given to the Big Bad Wolf himself. None of this would have been possible if he hadn't tried to eat me all those years ago. He was a great villain but is an even better rug.

And, of course, I'd like to thank *myself.* Very few monarchs have the brilliance, the beauty, the patience, the charisma, the bravery, and the tiaras to inspire history. Bravo, me!